With special thanks to Brandon Robshaw

For Toby Reid

ORCHARD BOOKS

First published in Great Britain in 2013 by The Watts Publishing Group

1 3 5 7 9 10 8 6 4 2

Text © 2013 Beast Quest Limited
Cover and inside illustrations by Artful Doodlers, with special thanks to Bob and Justin
© Beast Quest Limited 2013

Series created by Beast Quest Limited, London

A CIP catalogue record for this book is available from the British Library.

ISBN 978 1 40834 790 4

Printed in Great Britain

The paper and board used in this book are made from wood from responsible sources.

Orchard Books
An imprint of Hachette Children's Group
Part of The Watts Publishing Group Limited
Carmelite House, 50 Victoria Embankment, London EC4Y 0DZ

An Hachette UK Company
www.hachette.co.uk
www.hachettechildrens.co.uk

MANAK
THE SILENT PREDATOR

BY ADAM BLADE

ORCHARD

TEN YEARS EARLIER . . .

LOG BY: Niobe North
MISSION: Find the legendary city
             of Sumara
LOCATION: 1,603 fathoms deep.
             Co-ordinates unknown.

We don't have much time. This may be
the last entry I make. We're stuck
on the ocean bed and both engines
have failed.

The *Leaping Dolphin* is surrounded by
ocean crawlers. Hundreds of them.
They're attacking. They're scraping
at the hull. It's only a matter of
time before they break through.
Unless Dedrick can get the engines
started again, it's the end.

If this tape is ever found — if it
ever reaches you, Callum, and Max —
I want you to know I love you, and

>LOG ENTRY ENDS

CHAPTER ONE

HEADING NORTH

Max stood on the docks of the mighty city of Aquora. His mother held his left hand. His father held his right. Max's mother wore her pale green engineer overalls, and a light breeze stirred her long red hair. Max's dad stood tall and proud in his black Head Defence Engineer uniform. It was a warm, sunny day, and the sunlight sparkled on the ripples of the ocean.

I can't believe I'm back with Mum and Dad again, Max thought. *I was sure I'd lost them both forever!* He smiled at his mother. She smiled back, squeezing his hand.

"Where did you go?" he asked. "Why were you away for so long?"

"I've never been away, Max," she said. "I've always been with you."

Max turned to his father. "How did you get away? You were captured – kidnapped."

His father shook his head. "That never happened. It must have been a dream you had."

Max felt the ground under his feet tremble. Looking down, he saw the deck was splitting. A huge crack ran between him and his mother, widening rapidly. Their hands parted as they were pulled away from each other.

"Mum!"

Another crack appeared between him

and his father. Both his parents were holding out their hands to him – but the ground they stood on was moving away.

Max heard the crash and thud of falling masonry. Chunks of steel and glass and concrete tumbled into the sea, sending up huge splashes. Aquora was breaking up. His parents fell into the sea and disappeared beneath the waves.

"No!" Max cried. He stood on a floating piece of decking. It rocked and pitched beneath him, and then he was falling too, headlong into the ocean.

Max plunged beneath the waves. In the dark, icy water he saw the giant face of a man, with close-cropped grey hair, sharp, clever eyes and a cruel, laughing mouth. *I know that face*, he thought. *I know that man, but – who is he?*

The giant face opened its mouth. Instead

of a tongue, a slimy monster with tentacles emerged. It grabbed at Max's legs, pulling him further down into the ocean. He couldn't breathe.

Max struck at the creature with all his strength. But it was no good. A long, wet limb tightened around his chest—

"Aaagh!" he shouted.

His eyes snapped open. He looked around, trying to work out where he was. Slowly, he sat up.

He was in a giant conch shell, in an underwater cave. Lia was floating by the side of the shell, cradling a funny little fish in her arms. It was green, about the size of a kitten, with cute eyes and long whiskers sprouting from its jaws.

"It's a Whisker Fish," Lia said. "They're harmless. It only wanted to play." She stroked the Whisker Fish's head and

released it. It frisked away and was gone.

"Sorry," Max said. "I – I had a bad dream."

"How are you feeling now?" Lia said.

Max clambered out of the shell and stretched. "I'm OK," he said. "I guess I'm still feeling jumpy after everything we've been through. Getting caught in the undertow, and nearly eaten by Snapperfish, and having to fight two sea monsters – and I still don't know where my dad is."

"You'll feel better after eating," Lia said.

"I gathered some sea fungus while you were sleeping." She pointed at a plate-sized seashell on the seabed, filled with spongy red and green objects that looked like fancy mushrooms.

"Oh," Max said, feeling a slight sense of dread. So far, Merryn food hadn't exactly tickled his taste buds. "Is it – nice?"

"Delicious – and so good for you!"

A sense of doom descended over Max.

Lia picked up the shell. Spike, her pet swordfish, came nuzzling up to her. She fed him a couple of pieces and he snapped them up.

"OK, I'll try some," Max said. He picked up a piece of the sea fungus and chewed it.

"What do you think?" Lia asked.

"It's...unusual," Max said. Actually it tasted the way old socks probably did. He had no idea how Lia could call it delicious.

But there was nothing else to eat, and it would be rude to refuse it. He forced himself to eat a few more pieces.

"We'd better get moving," Max said when they finished eating. They had to find the next piece of the Skull of Thallos, stolen by the evil Professor. Without the Skull, the Merryn Aqua Powers were fading, and Lia's people would not be able to defend themselves against the Professor's plans to enslave them all and rule the ocean. But Max also had his own reason for wanting to defeat the Professor: he'd kidnapped Max's dad.

"Have you eaten enough?" Lia asked.

"Definitely," Max said.

He touched Rivet's head, and the dogbot, who had been in sleep mode, instantly awoke. His stumpy robot tail wagged from side to side. "Morning, Max. Morning, girl.

Morning, fish."

"Good boy, Rivet." Max opened the storage compartment in Rivet's back and retrieved the two-part piece of the Skull of Thallos that they had taken from the Robobeasts, Cephalox the Cyber Squid and Silda the Electric Eel. The pieces had fused together, as though they had never been separated, to form the lower half of the Skull. It glowed with a soft blue light. Max looked at the pointed jaw and the gaping eye-sockets and could hardly stop himself from shuddering.

He released the Skull. It floated in the water in front of him, then slowly turned and held steady.

"To the north!" Lia said.

"How do you know that way's north?" Max asked. "There's no sun down here to take your bearings from."

"I'm Merryn," Lia said. "We always know where we are in the sea."

Max got on his aquabike and revved the engine. Rivet paddled over to his side and Max returned the Skull to Rivet's back compartment. Lia sat astride Spike and led the way out of the cave.

Soon they were cruising through the ocean at top speed. They didn't speak much as they raced over undersea hills and valleys, past shoals of fish and fields of gently waving seaweed. Max was thinking about the clue they had found in the Professor's abandoned submarine – was it only yesterday? They now knew that the Professor's base was the Black Caves. And that must be where Max's dad was being held. But where in all the oceans of Nemos could the Black Caves be?

"Wait!" Lia said. She touched Spike's side to slow him down. Max hit the brakes.

"What?"

Lia looked worried. "If we keep going north, we'll reach the Forest of Souls."

"Is that bad?" Max asked.

"We mustn't go there unprepared!" Lia said. Abruptly, she swung Spike round and headed off.

"Where are you going?" called Max.

Lia shouted something over her shoulder, but Max couldn't hear what she said.

He twisted the throttle and raced to catch up with her. There was only one thought in his head now. *What is the Forest of Souls?*

CHAPTER TWO

ENTERING THE FOREST

Max saw Lia and Spike stop beside a huge black rock. He eased the aquabike to a halt by their side.

"What are you doing?" he asked.

"Watch." Lia made a piercing, whistling sound from the back of her throat. For a second, nothing happened. Then a host of little golden gleams of light shot out from cracks in the boulder – thousands of them, dancing round Max and Lia in a glittering swarm.

Max saw that they were tiny fish. Each was no longer than a joint in his finger, and they glowed different shades – some gold, some orange, some copper, some yellow, some almost white. He and Lia were standing in a sphere of shifting light.

The sparkles were reflected in Rivet's metal sides, and the sand on the ocean floor shone brilliant silver.

"Wow," Max said softly. "That's incredible."

Lia seemed pleased. "They're pretty, aren't they? They're called glindles."

"They're beautiful," Max said. "Thanks for showing them to me – only, do we have time for this? I mean, we're on a mission here."

"They'll light our way through the Forest of Souls," Lia said.

"Isn't there a danger that these...glindles will attract predators?"

Lia shook her head. "Absolutely not. Glindles give off a scent that repels other sea creatures. They will light the way and keep us safe from the creatures that lurk in the Forest of Souls."

Max felt a twinge of unease. "What creatures?"

"No one knows for sure," Lia said in a low voice, as if she feared someone was listening. "There are only rumours – legends. But it is said that dangerous monsters dwell there."

Max began to wonder if they would need something more than fish scent to get them safely through.

Lia made the whistling noise again, and the glindles followed her in a gleaming crowd as she steered Spike back towards the north.

Max rode beside her, enjoying the sensation of moving in a bubble of light. From time to time, Lia took scraps of kelp or fungus from her tunic and gave it to the glindles to nibble. Spike turned to look at her reproachfully, so she fed him too.

After a time, Max saw that Rivet was struggling – the poor dogbot wasn't built to keep up with Spike or the aquabike.

"Here, Rivet!" Max patted the space at the back of the bike. Rivet wagged his stumpy tail and jumped up behind Max.

He sat there, resting his propellers, as they rode further and further north.

Eventually, the scenery began to change. The dark green seaweed that was dotted about the ocean bed began to grow more thickly. The fronds grew taller – huge feathery arms that swayed in the ocean currents like the branches of trees in a breeze. Max began to feel hemmed in by the forest of dark, slimy seaweed that surrounded them, soaring far above their heads. If it hadn't been for the glindles, they would hardly have been able to see a thing.

"Is this it?" Max said. "The Forest of Souls?"

Lia inclined her head. "It is the beginning."

"Then let's check our bearings," Max said, wanting to be sure of their route.

He reached behind him and took out the Skull of Thallos from Rivet's storage compartment. He held it in front of him, and frowned. Something was wrong. The Skull wasn't glowing as steadily as before. Its light pulsed weakly, faded away, and then flared up briefly before fading away again.

He let go of it, watching to see where it pointed. But the Skull just bobbed in the water in front of him, slowly turning round, not settling on any direction.

"It's not working!" Max groaned. "Is that because we're in the Forest of Souls?"

"It must be," Lia said, in that same hushed voice she'd used earlier. "We must be very, very careful. No Merryn would enter this forest willingly."

Max felt like saying, *Neither would I*, but he stopped himself. If he wanted to be brave he had to sound brave. "It'll be fine," he said. "We know we're going in the right direction, and as long as we stick together we're bound to find some clue. If the Robobeast's hiding in here, we'll find it. We have the glindles, don't we?"

Lia nodded slowly. She patted Spike and they moved on. The fronds of seaweed became even thicker, pressing in on them.

Then, suddenly, they emerged into a clearing. Lia was ahead and Max heard her cry out in alarm. "Max!"

The next moment his own stomach twisted with fear.

Standing in the clearing, as if awaiting their arrival, was a green creature, the size of a man. There were frills around its lizard-like head. Beady black eyes stared straight at them and its mouth was twisted in an evil grin.

Max tensed. *This must be one of the creatures that live here*, he thought. *And if I have to fight my way past it...bring it on!*

CHAPTER THREE

BREAKING THE WAVES

"Go get him, Spike!" Lia yelled, and slapped the swordfish's flank.

Spike shot towards the creature. Max revved the aquabike and caught up – he couldn't let Lia face that thing alone.

Then he noticed that the creature wasn't moving. It stayed perfectly still, even when they were almost upon it. Max grabbed Lia's arm. "Wait!"

Lia pulled up Spike as Max hit reverse thrust.

The glindles cast their golden light around the figure, illuminating its green scaly skin and the feathery frills around its head. The grin was fixed on its face. It floated there, unmoving.

"It is alive – isn't it?" Lia said.

The figure's limbs stayed still, but Max

caught a tiny flicker of movement in its shiny black eyes. As if it was trying to communicate with them.

"It's definitely alive," he said. "But I think it's been paralysed."

Suddenly, the glindles shot off in different directions. Their light split into a thousand separate gleams. Darkness descended.

Lia called out in panic.

Something must have spooked the glindles. Max fumbled for the headlamps of the aquabike. He felt something hard butting him from behind, and turned. In the dim light he saw Rivet's square, metal head pushing against him.

"What is it, Rivet?" he asked. "What's got into you?"

"Something coming, Max!" replied the dogbot.

Max listened hard. He made out a low

humming from somewhere above, which was gradually getting louder. He'd never heard anything like it.

"We'd better hide," Max said to Lia, "until we see what it is."

They darted to the edge of the clearing and took shelter behind the dark fronds of seaweed. The humming grew louder. It sounded both musical and machine-like. A moment later, Max saw something descend from above. It was a large, green sphere, the size of a submarine. A pale yellow light spilled out from two round windows, like eyes.

"What is that?" Max whispered.

Lia shook her head. "I don't know. I've never seen anything like it."

The strange vessel stopped next to the paralysed figure, and the humming noise quietened. A hatch in the side opened,

and two more green, scaly figures swam out. They touched the motionless figure gently, and spoke low words in a language Max didn't understand. Then they took hold of their friend and pulled him aboard the green sphere. The hatch closed. The humming grew louder, and the vessel ascended towards the surface.

"Quick," Max said. "Let's follow it!"

"Why?" said Lia. "What does it have to do with our quest? I know now that Breathers can be brave, but this is madness!"

"We don't have any other clues – you want to just wander around here in the dark?"

"Those creatures could be dangerous!" she hissed.

"But they may be able to help us. They may know where the Robobeast is!"

"Well..." Lia said uncertainly. She bit her lip. "All right. As long as we're careful..."

"Of course," Max said. "Come on!"

Max twisted the throttle on his aquabike and pulled the handlebars up. Lia and Spike rose beside him, with Rivet paddling along gamely on the other side. The sphere was a long way above them, but it grew in size as they gained on it.

The water got lighter as they neared the

surface. So light that Max had to screw his eyes up. He had become used to the dim green shades of the undersea world.

There was a dark patch up on the surface, with tendrils that looked like roots dangling down from it. *Some sort of floating island, made of vegetation*, Max thought.

The vessel broke the surface. Max could see just the bottom half of it, bobbing in the water above. It moved towards the floating island, stopped and was hauled out of sight.

"Let's follow and see where they've gone!" Max said. The thought of seeing the sky and breathing air again filled him with excitement.

But Lia hung back. "I can't – I can't leave the ocean. I can't breathe air. No Merryn can. It's death to us."

"Wait a minute," Max said. He opened

the storage compartment of his aquabike and rummaged around. At last he pulled out an Amphibio mask – a lightweight oxygen mask with straps. "Put this on."

Lia shrank back. "What is it? Why do I have to cover my face?"

"Just try it," he told her.

"How does it work?" Lia asked.

"It delivers pure oxygen," he said, "just like you take from the water – no nitrogen in it. If you can breathe, put your thumb and first finger together in a circle, like this." He showed her the sign.

Hesitantly, Lia took the mask. Max helped her strap it on. Her eyes widened as she sucked in the oxygen. She smiled and made the circle sign.

Max pointed upwards. "If you can breathe through it under water, it'll be just the same up above."

He took her hand. Still she hung back, shaking her head.

"You'll be fine," Max said. "I promise. Trust me."

After a pause, Lia nodded. She kicked her legs and together they shot up to the surface.

Max gasped as his head broke through

the water. The sunlight was intense – diamond-white. The air felt incredibly clear and pure. It hurt his throat like an ice-cold drink. He was amazed at how easily his body moved out of the water, with no resistance to slow it down. *This must all seem so strange to Lia.* "Are you OK?" he asked.

She shielded her eyes from the light, and made the circle-sign again.

"Come on, then." They were close to the floating island – an enormous shaggy raft of seaweed. It rose from the water and they couldn't see what was on top. "Follow me!"

He floated free of his aquabike and swam the few strokes to the island, Lia swimming with him. Rivet and Spike stayed nearby, heads poking above the waves, watching them.

Max grabbed one of the woody tendrils

hanging from the side of the island and began to haul himself up.

Suddenly, something black and heavy landed on his shoulders with a thump. It was a tangle of thick ropes. Max shouted and struggled, but the ropes tightened around him. He glanced over his shoulder and saw that Lia was gathered into the net with him. He felt the net being pulled upwards, and heard grunts and panting. The tough stems of plants scraped against his body as they were dragged up onto the island.

Max looked up through the gaps in the net, to see two of the green men from earlier standing over him. Their black eyes stared down, their frilly, lizard-like heads framed by brilliant blue sky. They were grinning. One of them bent to Max and pushed a spongy, sweet-smelling pad over his face. He thrashed and tried to pull the

scaly hand away, but it was too strong. He breathed in and the strong fumes stung his lungs. His brain reeled.

Then everything went black.

CHAPTER FOUR

A CIRCLE OF FRIENDS

Max opened his eyes. He was lying on his back in darkness. He pushed out his arms, expecting to move through water, but nothing happened. He was breathing air through his nose. As his eyes got used to the dimness, he saw that he was lying on a bed in a small hut, with green walls. A bright line of sunlight marked out the edges of the doorframe.

Where was Lia?

He sat up and winced as a fierce pain lanced through his skull. He sat still for a while, waiting for the moment to pass. He touched the wall of the hut behind him – it was hard, slightly bumpy and smelt of the sea. Dried, toughened seaweed, he realised.

The door burst open. Two of the scaly green creatures poked their heads in.

"What have you done with Lia?" Max demanded.

They shouted something he couldn't understand and rushed towards him.

He thrust out his hands to fend them off – but they grabbed him by the ankles and hauled him from the bed. Max hit the floor with a sickening thud. His stomach churned. He threw his arms around his head to protect himself as he was dragged from the hut and bumped over the ground.

The sun, high overhead, was painfully bright.

They reached a clear, flat area in the open, where Max's captors let him go. He struggled to his feet. He was in a space with a smooth green floor, a kind of public square or meeting place. More of the scaly green creatures came to circle him, murmuring in a strange language.

Max tensed his muscles, ready to defend himself if necessary. "I haven't done anything!" he said in the Merryn language. "What do you want with me? Where's Lia?"

They didn't answer, but murmured to each other more loudly.

The ring of figures parted, and two more of the scaly beings appeared, carrying Lia with her arms over their shoulders. Max saw with relief that she was still wearing the silver oxygen mask.

They sat her down. She got up at once, stumbled towards Max and stood close by him. He did his best to give her a reassuring smile.

"Are you all right?" he asked.

She frowned and rubbed her brow. "I have a headache," she murmured.

"Me too," he said. "But at least they

left your mask on – they obviously want us alive." *For the time being, anyway*, he thought.

The green figures pressed in closer, peering at them curiously. *As if we were the strange ones*, Max thought, *not them*. But then, Max remembered, Lia had looked strange to him the first time they'd met.

"Why have you captured us?" Lia demanded. The Amphibio mask muffled her voice. "And what have you done with Spike and Rivet?"

One of the scaly people, who Max thought looked older than the rest, stepped forwards and spread his arms.

"I am sorry," he said, in a soft, creaky voice, "we do not understand your language." With a jolt of surprise, Max realised he understood. He glanced at

Lia, and saw from the blankness of her face that she hadn't.

Only then did Max get it – the scaly figure had spoken in human language! Max gaped at him.

"Do either of you speak the human tongue?" the scaly person asked.

"Yes – me – I do!" said Max. He hadn't spoken human for a while, and the words felt odd and clunky in his mouth. "Who are you, and what do you want with us?"

"You followed us and came onto our island," the older man said. "What do *you* want with *us*?"

"We meant no harm," Max said. "We are on a quest, and we need help. I am Max, and this is my friend, Lia."

Lia plucked at his arm. "What are you saying?"

"I'll tell you in a minute," Max whispered.

"I think we're going to be all right, though. He seems reasonable."

The elderly person bowed. "I am Lang'onol, the elder of our tribe."

"How do you know human language so well?" Max asked.

"I have studied the language and customs of many peoples – though not, I regret to say, the Merryn." He inclined his head to Lia, and she stared back at him. "Most of our people are peaceful scholars like me," he continued. "Our name, in the human language, means the Curious Ones – we are the Szurt'zjan'kroy."

"The... Shirtskoy?" Max said uncertainly.

The scaly people laughed. It sounded unexpectedly bright and high-pitched.

"Not quite," Lang'onol said gravely. "Though it was a good try. You may call us the Kroy, for short."

"Ask him why they netted us and knocked us out!" Lia hissed. "Tell him I am a Princess and not used to such treatment!"

"Err…" Max said, wondering how best to put this.

"Your companion is asking about the rough way we treated you, I would guess?" Lang'onol said. "For this we apologise. We had to be sure you were not enemies. We are perhaps a suspicious people by nature, but recent events have made us more so."

"Recent events?" Max said, suddenly alert. Perhaps his instinct had been right – maybe these people could offer some sort of clue to help them on their quest.

"Our home has always been in the Forest of Souls, below the sea – and we have lived for many generations there in peace. We know that dark stories are told about the

Forest of Souls, among peoples such as the Merryn – this suited us well, for it kept unwanted visitors away. But something has come to our homeland which truly is dark. That is why we have made our home on the Floating Island."

"What was it?" Max asked. He was beginning to feel this might have something to do with the Professor.

"A deadly creature, that we call Manak, the Silent Predator. It glides close to the ocean floor, without a sound. When it finds prey, it strikes with venom, which paralyses."

Max remembered the motionless figure the Kroy had rescued from the ocean bed. "So – that Kroy person we saw you take into your vessel – is he...?"

"That was Zarn'ol. He descended to the Forest of Souls to see if it was safe yet to return. And Manak struck. Luckily we reached Zarn'ol in time – we have medicine to counteract the venom, and he will recover. An hour later, and it would have been too late."

Max was feeling more and more sure that the Silent Predator must be one of the Professor's Robobeasts. "This Manak – does it have any sort of robotics attached to it?"

Lang'onol's forehead creased in puzzlement. "Robotics?"

"You know," Max said, "like – machinery – metal bits, plugged into it?"

Lang'onol shook his head. "We have seen no such thing," he told Max. "Manak is a demon of the deep – he is no machine."

Max explained to Lia, in Merryn, what Lang'onol had said. "That must be the next Robobeast, don't you think?" he asked.

"Then why does it have none of the Professor's technology on it?" Lia asked.

"I don't know," Max said. "But it's the closest thing we have to a clue." He turned back to Lang'onol and said: "We are on a quest to find and defeat this monster. Lia and I will descend to the Forest of Souls to find it. Can any of your people guide us?"

Lang'onol looked grave. He translated Max's request for his people. There was a murmuring and a shuffling of feet. Max could hardly blame them for not leaping forward – they must be remembering what had happened to Zarn'ol.

At last a small boy pushed through the crowd. His skin was pale green and smooth. He said something in the Kroy language, and some of the crowd cheered and laughed. Max and Lia exchanged glances. Surely this boy, hardly more than

an infant, wasn't going to guide them?

Another Kroy, an adult, hurriedly
stepped out. He grasped the boy by his

shoulders and gently moved him back.

"My son shames me," he said. "I won't let him go." He turned to Max. "I'll go instead."

CHAPTER FIVE

VENOM

"I am Tusc'ol." He reached out and touched Max's fingertips. *This must be how the Kroy greet each other*, Max guessed. Tusc'ol touched Lia's fingertips too, and then abruptly started walking away.

"Where are you going?" Max said.

Tusc'ol spoke over his shoulder. "We must go now, not wait. We must do this, so let's do it quick."

That sounded like good sense to Max.

"Come on," he said to Lia, and they quickly caught Tusc'ol up.

"We wish you well!" Lang'onol called.

Tusc'ol led them across the island. It was made entirely of dried seaweed and felt springy to walk on. There were streets of dark green dwellings, much bigger than the hut Max had been confined in, all made of seaweed. They soon reached the edge of the island. Waves lapped against a low pier where Max's aquabike was tied up alongside the spherical vessel that had rescued Zarn'ol.

"Max!" came a familiar bark. "Hello, Max!"

Rivet came scooting out from behind the aquabike, his propellers churning and his tail wagging. At the same moment, Spike's long snout broke through the waves.

"Spike!" Lia shouted in delight. She tore

off her mask and dived straight into the sea. As soon as she surfaced she hugged Spike, who nuzzled up against her.

Max picked up the Amphibio mask. He knelt at the edge of the pier and patted Rivet's head. "Good boy, Rivet! It's great to see you again!"

"We must go," Tusc'ol said shortly. He walked straight off the end of the jetty and plunged feet first into the water.

Max climbed aboard the bobbing aquabike, put the oxygen mask in the storage compartment and untied the rope. "Come on, Rivet!" he said. Then he tilted the aquabike forward and plunged beneath the waves, entering the dim green undersea world once more.

Max felt the pressure of the sea enclosing him again, and the coolness of the water flowing through his gills. He saw Lia up

ahead, sitting astride Spike. Beyond,
Tusc'ol pointed downwards, then neatly
flipped head over heels and began to swim
with powerful strokes towards the ocean
bed. He was fast. Max twisted the throttle
to catch up with him. Lia and Spike came

alongside, with Rivet bringing up the rear.

The water got darker and darker as they descended. Soon the topmost fronds of the Forest of Souls were brushing against them. Still they carried on going down, through ever thicker fronds. They pushed against Max's body as if trying to grab him.

"Are we nearly at the bottom?" Max asked.

Tusc'ol didn't answer, just pointed downwards and carried on swimming.

Max started as a big, pale dead fish floated past, belly up. He and Lia exchanged glances.

"Manak's work," Tusc'ol said.

"Don't worry, Spike," Lia said, patting the swordfish's head. "I won't let it get you."

Max scanned the dark fronds around him, and strained his ears to hear any telltale sounds of movement. But he remembered that Lang'onol had said that Manak made no sound. The Silent Predator. *If Manak attacks*, Max thought, *I won't hear anything until it's too late...*

At last the ocean floor loomed before them. It was dark, smooth, and very slightly mottled – the natural marbling of the rock, Max supposed. Tusc'ol flipped over and landed feet-first. He pointed at Max's aquabike and put his finger to his lips. "Switch off. No noise."

Max eased off the throttle. Lia, on Spike, came to a stop beside him. A few moments later, Rivet arrived, paddling gamely.

Tusc'ol set off, and beckoned for them to follow. Max opened the bike's pannier and took out his hyperblade. It was a curved weapon of pure vernium – the hardest metal known to the scientists of Aquora. The blade was paper-thin, but

unbreakable, and sharp enough to slice through anything. He felt slightly more confident with a weapon in his hand – it was a small thing against a giant, venomous monster, but at least it was something. He wouldn't use his blade to attack, only to protect himself. He was about to slip off the aquabike when Rivet gave a loud bark.

"Shush, Rivet!" Lia said.

"Something must have spooked him,"

Max said. "What is it, Rivet?'

Max caught a movement out of the corner of his eye.

The next instant, he saw an enormous black whip rear out of the darkness ahead. Before any of them had time to move, it hit Tusc'ol in the chest, like a striking snake.

Tusc'ol barely cried out. He stiffened immediately and stood unmoving, paralysed by the venom. His face was frozen into a mask of horror.

"Tusc'ol!" Lia cried out.

"It must be Manak!" Max said. He gripped his hyperblade tighter. "Where is he?"

He and Lia peered around them tensely, alert for another movement. There was no sound whatsoever. Tusc'ol started to drift upwards from the seabed. He was still frozen in the mid-stride position he'd been in when Manak struck. Max felt his nerves stretched to breaking point.

Suddenly, the floor shifted beneath him. Max saw Lia's eyes widen in fear – she'd felt it too. He looked down and saw the sand sliding on the smooth dark rock, except at that moment he realised it wasn't rock at all.

"Lia!" Max cried. "We...we're—" He could hardly get the words out.

"We're standing on Manak," his friend said.

CHAPTER SIX

SACRIFICE

"We have to move!" Max shouted. "Get away from its sting."

He gunned the engine of the aquabike and shot forwards. Next to him, Lia plunged ahead on Spike, with Rivet bringing up the rear.

Manak was a broad, flat, dark shape beneath them. Far ahead, Max could see a raised bump. *That must be its head*, he thought. *That's probably where the robotic control harness is – and the next piece of the Skull of Thallos! If I can just reach it...*

But Manak was gliding beneath them, silently keeping pace. They weren't getting any closer to its head.

They passed through a denser part of the Forest of Souls where the seaweed grew more thickly. *Maybe the plants will slow it down*, Max thought.

But they didn't. Manak brushed the thick seaweed fronds aside as though they weren't there. Some of the stems were as thick as tree trunks, but they bent right back as Manak glided through.

Max realised how powerful the monster was. *Impossible to defeat*, he thought. But he banished the idea from his head at once. He had to fight Manak – and win!

The forest thinned out again as they came to a clearing. The water was lighter here and for the first time Max got a proper look at Manak. It was a giant stingray, its great wings spreading far away on each side. The whip that had paralysed Tusc'ol had to be the monster's tail. Up ahead, Max saw the rounded hump at the centre of the two wings more clearly, and spotted two eye-bumps sticking up. That was definitely the head area, but he saw no sign of any harness or robotics, no glint of metal. Had he got it wrong? Maybe this wasn't one of the Professor's Robobeasts – just a terrible underwater monster.

"Max! Look out!" Lia screamed.

Max turned and saw Manak's tail whipping towards him at lightning speed. He swerved the aquabike and veered off to the side. The tip of the tail missed him by a fraction.

He twisted the throttle, trying to get further away from the deadly sting – but the bike wouldn't go any faster.

Again the tail lashed through the water, this time towards Lia. She ducked. The sting passed so close to her head that Max saw her long silver hair sway in the current it made.

We have to do something! Max thought. But what? They couldn't keep this up – Manak looked as if it would never tire, and they wouldn't be able to escape that lethal sting forever.

A dangling frond of seaweed loomed up before Max and he had to swerve round it. A moment later, Manak's tail sliced through the water, aimed at where he had been an instant before. It slashed right through the tough seaweed as if it was paper. Max saw that its tail was covered with shining metal, and his heart leapt – that had to be the Professor's work! But still he saw no sign of a robotic harness. The Professor always controlled his monsters with a harness – or he had, until now. If Max couldn't find that, how could he stop the Robobeast?

"Max!" Lia called. "Remember Cephalox!"

"What?"

"You remember, when you—" Her words were cut short as she veered to one side, avoiding another lash of Manak's sting. But she didn't need to say any more – Max realised suddenly what she meant. When they had fought Cephalox the Cyber Squid, he had tricked it into smashing its own harness with its tentacle. Max had darted out of the way and Cephalox hadn't been able to stop from striking its own body. Could Max pull the same trick on Manak now? *If I can make it sting itself, its own venom might paralyse it!*

At least, that was what Max hoped.

He slowed the aquabike down so that he was closer to Manak's tail end, deliberately making himself an easier target.

"Come and get me, Manak!" he shouted.

Immediately, the venomous tail whipped towards him. Max steered left. But instead of striking Manak's body, the tail adjusted, bending like a water-snake, and followed him. The tip of the tail struck the back of Max's aquabike so hard it almost jolted him off it.

This was a dangerous game – if the sting had been a hair's breadth closer he'd have

been paralysed. But he couldn't give up. *This is my only hope*, he thought.

Again he steered the aquabike towards Manak's tail, keeping close to the beast's body.

This time it seemed as if Manak had been expecting the move – the tail lashed at Max even faster than before. He swerved frantically. But he could see the deadly, metal-edged tail following him. He couldn't escape. Lia screamed a warning. A blur of silver appeared at the corner of his eye.

Crash!

Max heard metal clashing on metal, close to his head, and saw a dazzling burst of sparks. For a second he had no idea what had happened. Then he saw Rivet somersaulting through the water. The dogbot's eyes had gone dead and his

propellers weren't moving.

Max realised what had happened: Rivet
had swum in between him and Manak's

sting and knocked it off course. The giant ray's venom couldn't hurt him – but the tail must be electric as well as venomous. It had blown Rivet's circuits. He had sacrificed himself to save Max.

Max felt sick. He would do anything to bring Rivet back to life.

But first he had to stay alive himself.

CHAPTER SEVEN
LIFE OR DEATH

Max forced himself to think calmly. There was nothing he could do about Rivet right now. First, he had to defeat Manak. The monster was one of the Professor's Robobeasts – the steel tail proved that. So the robotic control harness that held the piece of the Skull of Thallos must be on it somewhere. It had to be.

He pulled the handlebars of the aquabike towards him and roared upwards, leaving Rivet's lifeless form to float down to rest on the ocean bed.

Lia rose and appeared beside him, on Spike.

"What are you doing?" she asked.

"Looking," he told her. From this height, Max could see Manak in its entirety. At last he got a true sense of how enormous the Robobeast was. Its dark, mottled shape seemed to cover half the ocean floor. But Max couldn't see the glint of metal or white bone, anywhere. It was impossible that the robotic attachment could be fixed to Manak's sides – the creature was so flat it barely had any sides. Which meant…

Of course! Max thought.

The robotics and the harness must be underneath Manak. On its underbelly. Tucked out of harm's way. That made sense. And if he could just get under the stingray he'd have a chance of finding the equipment and detaching it.

Just get under the stingray. Easier said than done...

Ahead of Manak, Max saw a hollow in the ocean floor – a natural dip in the rock, just deep enough for a person or two to hide in. This looked like his chance.

"Lia, can you do something to distract Manak – keep it busy?"

"Why? What are you going to do?" she asked.

Max pointed at the hollow. "I'm going down there," he said.

Lia nodded. "Leave it to us!" She patted Spike's side. "Come on, Spike!"

Max pushed the handles of the aquabike down, and dived at full throttle towards Manak. The creature's dark, mottled hide seemed to rush up to meet him. He levelled out just above the monster's back. As he shot a glance behind him he saw that Lia and Spike had also descended. Spike was slashing at Manak's back with his sword-like bill. Lia was scraping at the creature's hide with a razor-clam shell she must have picked up.

Spike's sword and Lia's shell wouldn't really injure a creature Manak's size – but the attack was distracting it. It slowed down and its whole back vibrated. Its tail came sweeping round at its attackers. Lia ducked and Spike darted to one side. The tail only just missed.

Max gunned the aquabike again and headed straight down the monster's middle, towards the head. He shot between Manak's eyes – two blank pale bumps, near the front end. Then he had overtaken the stingray. He dived down into the hollow and slammed on the brakes.

The world grew dark as Max's enemy passed above. Max flicked the aquabike's lights on. Overhead, Manak's underbelly slid by – a white wall of solid muscle. Max stood on the bike, straining to see the telltale glint of the metal harness that held the robotic control panel in place.

Yes! There it was, plugged into Manak's underbelly, rushing towards him.

He had one chance to get this – miss, and the Robobeast would be gone.

He put his hyperblade between his teeth, leapt and grabbed the harness with both hands.

The jolt nearly pulled his arms out of their sockets. Instantly he was being whipped along at breathtaking speed. He needed a free hand to reach the control panel. He held tight to the harness strut with one hand and let go with the other. The strain on his arm made him want to cry out. He bit tighter on the hyperblade, feeling it scrape against his teeth. With the other hand he scrabbled at the metal cover of the control panel. It wouldn't budge.

Max took the hyperblade in his fist. He

thrust the weapon into the gap at the edge of the cover.

Manak bucked violently. It must have felt the pressure of the blade. It carried on jerking, doing its best to shake Max off.

Max's arm ached and his fingers felt as if they were breaking. But he held fast. The Robobeast's movements jogged the hyperblade out of position. Max gritted his teeth and tried again, stabbing the super-fine blade into the narrow gap.

The monster swam lower. Max felt the rocky ocean floor bumping against him. He cried out in pain as stones scraped at his knees. Manak was trying to knock him off. A sharp rock hit him in the back and he only just managed to hold on. He could feel his grip weakening...

A fierce determination burned in Max's heart – he wouldn't give in. He wouldn't

let the Professor beat him! He attacked the
cover with new strength, and felt it give. At
last it came loose, fell and was left behind.

Max saw the control panel, with its array
of buttons, and just above it the white
gleam of the Skull, held by metal bands.

Up ahead, he saw a huge boulder rushing
towards him. Any second now, he would
smash into it with bone-crushing force. If he
let go he could save himself – but he wouldn't
get another chance at the control panel.

He had to work fast.

He hacked at the panel with the hyperblade, blindly, madly, with every bit of strength he possessed.

Crunch!

He felt the panel splinter into fragments, and saw the shard of white bone drift free from its moorings.

Manak swam on, just above the seabed. The boulder was right in front. Max braced himself for the impact. The monster suddenly rose up, as if it had woken from a dream. It seemed to have forgotten all about hurting Max.

The stingray is free of the Professor's curse, Max thought. He'd liberated another sea creature.

Max let go and tumbled to the ocean floor, skidding along, gradually losing speed. He came to rest against

the boulder with a bump.

Shakily, Max got to his feet. The Skull of Thallos floated through the water towards him. He reached up and grabbed it. Max didn't feel like celebrating though. Instead his first thought was of Rivet. *Where's my dogbot?*

He swam back to his aquabike. It was still where he'd left it, in the hollow. He jumped on and headed back the way he'd come. The headlights lit up the dark fronds of seaweed. How was he ever going to find Rivet here?

I hope Lia's all right too, he thought. *I hope Manak's sting didn't get her.*

"Lia!" he called. But there was no answer.

Max nosed the aquabike slowly through the seaweed fronds, scanning the sand and rocks of the ocean floor. Suddenly his heart jumped as he saw Rivet's metal body lying on its side, half hidden by kelp.

He dismounted and crouched down by his dogbot. Rivet's eyes were black and lifeless.

"Rivet!" Max said. The dogbot's ears didn't prick up as they were programmed to do. Max opened up the control panel on Rivet's back, and saw that the hyper-conductors inside were blackened and twisted. The stingray's tail had short-circuited Rivet. If he rewired him, Max could get the current flowing again and his dogbot would reawaken. But he had to act fast – Rivet's memory would be deleted if he was inactive for more than an hour.

Max cut the old hyper-conductors away with his hyperblade, and began to search in Rivet's storage compartment for new ones.

"Max!" he heard Lia shout, and felt a burst of relief. She was all right! Lia and Spike swam towards him. "We must go back."

"Wait," he said, grinning at her with

relief. "I'm just working on Rivet here."

Spike swam up and nuzzled against Rivet, as if trying to wake him.

"We can't worry about him now!" Lia said.

"We have to," Max said. "If I don't fix him fast, it'll be too late to bring him back to life as he was – all his memory will be wiped."

"'But we have to get Tusc'ol back to his people," Lia said. "Otherwise it will be too late to cure him. He'll die!"

CHAPTER EIGHT

RETURN TO LIFE

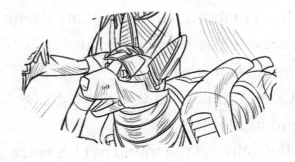

Max knew Lia was right. Tusc'ol had risked his life to bring them here, and he had family, a son... However much Max cared about his dogbot, it was more important to save Tusc'ol than Rivet.

Max hoisted Rivet onto the aquabike, and he and Lia raced back to the place where they had first encountered Manak. Tusc'ol could be anywhere in this shadowy forest of seaweed.

"Let's split up," Lia said. "More chance of finding him." She and Spike darted into the thick of the forest.

Max cruised around and up and down on his aquabike. The headlights shone on the seaweed as he passed, turning it from green to yellow.

"Come quick!" Lia shouted. "Spike's found him!"

Max followed the sound of Lia's voice and found her. Spike was pointing up with his sword. The paralysed figure drifted among the seaweed fronds. Max and Lia rose up and each took hold of an arm, bearing him along between them, Lia on Spike and Max on his aquabike.

Soon they were nearing the surface. The water became lighter.

Lia started to look concerned. "I can't go back into the air, I threw the mask

away," she admitted.

Max reached into the container of the aquabike. "Is this what you're looking for?" He handed her the Amphibio mask. "What would you do without me?"

Lia smiled and put the mask on.

They broke the surface near the pier. A crowd of the Kroy were waiting for them, and when they saw Max and Lia they started cheering. But the cheers died away as they saw the motionless figure of Tusc'ol.

Hands reached out to take hold of Tusc'ol and lift him onto the pier. An old Kroy, wearing a white robe, bent and examined him. He said something in a low voice, and four other Kroy quickly raised Tusc'ol and carried him away. The elder followed.

Max and Lia scrambled on to the Floating Island, helped by the Kroy. Max held Rivet's unmoving body in his arms. Spike poked his head out of the water and watched as Rivet was taken onto the island. Max could have sworn the swordfish looked anxious.

"You encountered the Silent Predator, then," Lang'onol said.

"Yes – it won't trouble you ever again," Max said. "But it hurt Tusc'ol. Will he… Is he going to be all right?"

"Time will tell," Lang'onol replied. "He

has been taken to the healer's hut. All we can do is wait – and hope."

He turned and walked inside one of the larger green huts. An anxious crowd had gathered outside.

Max put Rivet down and knelt to open his storage compartment. He took out some hyper-conductors and quickly trimmed them to the right length. Then he opened Rivet's control panel and fitted them into position, twisting them so they stayed in contact with the conductors. He pressed the 'Recharge' button, closed the control panel and sat back on his heels to wait, trying not to think about how he'd feel if this didn't work.

"Will he wake?" Lia asked. She was leaning over his shoulder to watch.

"I hope so. He risked his life to save me," Max said. He felt a lump in his throat.

"Didn't you, Rivet?"

There was a pause. Still Rivet didn't move. *That's it, then*, Max thought dully. *He's gone. The shock must have been too powerful.*

Rivet's tail wagged feebly. His eyes glowed. There was a whirring sound.

Relief flooded over Max. "You're alive!"

"Max!" Rivet barked. "Alive, Max!" He rolled and stood upright on his four metal

paws. His tail wagged strongly.

Lia put her hand on Max's shoulder. "I'm so glad."

"Me too," Max said. If he'd lost Rivet, he wasn't sure he could have gone on.

A shout went up from the Kroy. Max and Lia ran towards the healer's hut. The crowd parted as the door of the hut opened. The healer came out in his long white robe – and with him was Tusc'ol, still unsteady on his feet but alive and well. Tusc'ol's little boy ran to him and hugged him.

The Kroy cheered and raised their hands in the air. Max and Lia joined in. But as Max looked at Lia's raised arms he saw that one of them had a long, bloody wound running up it. He felt as if someone had thrown iced water over him.

"What's that?" he demanded.

Lia frowned. "It's where Manak's tail cut

me," she said. "When you were under the monster, and I was distracting it. Don't worry – it's just a scratch."

It looked much worse than a scratch to Max. He felt terrible for not having noticed it earlier. "You need to get that looked at," Max said.

"It's fine," said Lia. "I'm not paralysed, am I?"

Max ignored her and waved a hand to get the attention of the Kroy healer. "Excuse me? Could you take a look at this?"

The elder came over. He examined Lia's wound carefully and wiped it with a sponge. "It does not seem infected. We must leave it to heal."

"Can't you use any of your medicines on it?" Max asked. "Just in case...?"

The old man shook his head. "Kroy medicine is not made for Merryn. The effects might be dangerous. Better to leave it. I do not think venom has entered the wound. You can see she is not paralysed. How do you feel?" he asked Lia.

Max translated for his friend.

"Tell him I feel well," she said. "We need to press on with our quest."

"I will bandage the wound," the healer said, "in case the blood should attract sharks."

He gently wrapped a pale green bandage, made of dried, softened seaweed, around Lia's arm.

Lang'onol came up to them. "We cannot thank you enough for freeing us from the menace of the Silent Predator. Now we can return to our home in the Forest of Souls, where we will hold a great feast to celebrate. We hope you will attend as our honoured guests."

Max quickly told Lia what Lang'onol had said and a smile spread across her face.

"Thank you," Max said to Lang'onol. "But we must go. Don't worry, we'll keep the legend that the Forest of Souls is haunted, so your people won't be troubled by travellers."

The elder smiled down at Max. "I know the human word for you," he said, planting a hand on Max's shoulder. "They call people like you 'hero.'"

CHAPTER NINE
A MESSAGE

The Kroy stood at the edge of the floating island and waved farewell as Max and Lia slipped beneath the waves.

Underwater, Spike rubbed the end of his nose against Rivet's square metal snout. Rivet wagged his tail.

They set off, descending to the Forest of Souls again. Once they were deep among the seaweed fronds, Max slowed his aquabike and took out the Skull of Thallos from Rivet's back storage compartment.

He fitted the third piece on and it clicked into place as if attracted by a magnet. There was a flash of blue light, and then the Skull gave off a steady glow. The third piece was the beak. Now there was just one piece missing – the rear part. Max released the Skull. It turned in the water and pointed to the side, directing them out of the Forest of Souls.

"It's working again, then," Max said.

Lia nodded. "Now that the influence of

Manak has gone, the Skull of Thallos seeks its missing part. The final part."

They headed in the direction the Skull pointed.

After a while, the seaweed forest began to thin out. The Forest of Souls had made Max feel claustrophobic, and he looked forward to being back in open water again. They came out through the last few bits of seaweed. The wide ocean stretched out before them.

Max drew in his breath. Ahead of them was a thin, pale figure, floating there beyond the final bits of seaweed as if waiting for them. Max touched Lia's arm.

"Watch out – there's someone there," he said. "Looks like they're lying in wait."

But to Max's surprise, Lia's eyes lit up. "Glave!" she called. She urged Spike on and moved swiftly towards the figure.

Max followed. Glave was a teenaged Merryn, tall, slim and bony, with dark, hollow eyes. Lia was already embracing him.

"This is my cousin!" she said.

Max and Glave nodded at each other.

"But Glave, where have you been?" Lia demanded. "We thought you'd gone for good. We thought the Professor had got you."

"He did get me," Glave said, in a flat voice.

As if he doesn't want to think about it, Max thought.

"I was out food-gathering," Glave continued, "and had strayed further from Sumara than usual. I was seized by the Professor's aquadrones."

"Aquadrones?" Max said, puzzled. "What are they?"

"The Professor's robot servants," said Glave. "They took me and made me work in the Professor's factories in the Black Caves."

"Couldn't you escape?" Lia asked.

Glave gave an empty laugh. "Escape? The Black Caves are guarded by attack bots. Not to mention the most terrifying monster in all the ocean – Kraya the Blood Shark."

"But you're out now," Max said.

"The Professor let me out," Glave said. "He ordered me to deliver a message. He said that I would find you here, at the edge of the Forest of Souls. The message is for a Breather named Max."

"That's me," Max said, revving his aquabike and moving closer to Glave. "What's the message?"

"It's here," Glave said. "In this box."

He handed Max a square metal case. Rivet swam to the box and sniffed it curiously. "What is it, Max?" barked the dogbot.

Max inspected it. "It's an Aquora submarine DiveLog – submariners use it to record their voyages."

But where could the Professor have got hold of it? Max wondered. *And why did he want me to have it? How did he even know I'd be here at this moment?*

Max felt a tingling sensation of unease. He had a feeling that whatever message was in the DiveLog, it wouldn't be good news.

He turned it over and his heart somersaulted as he saw the image of a leaping dolphin. It was the mark of the submarine that had taken his mother and uncle on their voyage into the ocean – a voyage from which they had never returned.

"What is?" Lia asked. "What is the message?"

The DiveLog had earphones attached. Max inserted the earphones, and pressed the 'Activate' button.

CHAPTER TEN

MIND GAMES

Max hadn't heard his mother's voice since he was an infant, except in dreams, but the voice that filled his ears now seemed the most familiar sound in the world.

She was breathless. Frightened. "We don't have much time," Max's mother said. "This may be the last entry I make. We're stuck on the ocean bed and both engines have failed."

In the background, Max heard clanging

and scraping noises, and a man's voice – his uncle's – too remote for Max to make out actual words. He sounded desperately anxious.

"The *Leaping Dolphin* is surrounded by ocean crawlers," his mother said. "Hundreds of them."

Max's skin prickled – ocean crawlers were crablike creatures with snapping pincers which travelled in swarms and ate everything in their path. Max had never seen one, but he'd heard about them and they'd haunted his nightmares when he was younger. He'd thought they were fairy-tale monsters – stories to scare children with at bedtime. But then, he'd thought that about the Merryn too, and they had turned out to be real.

"They're attacking," his mother went on. Her voice was sounding more desperate. "They're scraping at the hull. It's only a matter of time before they break through. Unless Dedrick can get the engines started again, it's the end." Max heard his mother gulp back a sob. "If this tape is ever found – if it ever reaches you, Callum, and Max – I want you to know I love you, and—"

Max's uncle's voice rose to a ragged yell. There were louder clangs, the sound of metal being torn, a torrent of water.

A scream from his mother.

Then a thud, and a long hiss of static.

Then silence.

Slowly, Max pulled out the headphones. Over the years, he had accepted the belief that his mother was dead. Yet, always, there had been a small, lingering hope that she might somehow have survived. Now that was gone forever.

"What was it?" Lia asked. "What was the message?"

"My mother," said Max, shortly. He didn't want to talk about it. "Her last words, before the ocean crawlers...before they—"

Lia put her hand gently on his shoulder. "I'm so sorry," she said.

"Thanks," Max said. He rubbed his fists in his eyes.

"Why did the Professor send you this message?"

Max shook his head. "No idea. Perhaps just to hurt me. Anyway…" He took a deep breath and raised his chin. "Talking of the Professor, he still has my dad. Let's get going. I lost my mother, but maybe I can still save my father."

"Which way is it to the Black Caves?" Lia asked Glave. "And how far?"

"About a hundred leagues," Glave said. He pointed. "To the north-west."

"Thank you," Lia said. "Now you must

go back to Sumara, with all the speed you have. Your mother and father are worried sick about you. They will be so happy and relieved at your return!"

"Yes," Glave said, and smiled. Max saw some life come into his face at the thought of going home. It was as if he had only just realised his captivity was over.

"Tell them in Sumara that we're going to defeat the Professor for good!" Max said. "Tell them that when we come back the ocean will be safe again."

"I wish you all the luck that Thallos can send!" Glave said, and with a final wave he swam off towards Sumara.

Max and Lia set off side by side, in the direction of the Black Caves. Max's mind was buzzing. Why had the Professor sent Glave to them? He must have known that Lia's cousin would direct them towards his lair. It was as if the Professor was luring them to him.

And how did the Professor get hold of the DiveLog? Why did he send it to Max? How did he even know it had anything to do with Max? How did he know who Max's mother was? Their enemy seemed to know more than it was possible for him to know.

Unless... A thought stirred, half-formed, in Max's mind. *Unless the Professor is...*

"What are you thinking about?" Lia asked.

"I'm thinking that I can't wait to come face to face with the Professor," Max said. "And anything he can throw at us."

He gunned the engine of the aquabike and accelerated, so that Rivet and Lia and Spike had to put on speed to keep up. Together they forged through the ocean, drawing ever closer to the Black Caves.

*I'm not going to let the Professor's mind
games get to me, Max thought. Nothing is
going to stop me rescuing my dad!*

In the next Sea Quest
adventure, Max must face

KRAYA
THE BLOOD SHARK

Read on for an exclusive extract...

Bright blue light burst out and made him blink. "Wow!" said Max. He opened his eyes a crack and took out the glowing Skull of Thallos. The three fragments – a jawbone, eye-sockets and beak – were magically fused together. Each piece had pointed the way to the next, but they'd never glowed this brightly before.

"We must be really close," said Lia.

"I don't understand," said Max. "There's nothing around—"

A deep rumble from the seabed drowned his words and he felt the water pulse. "What in the seven seas is that?" he asked, quickly stowing away the Skull.

"I don't know," said Lia, "but I don't think we should stay here. Spike!"

The ocean shook again.

"Go up!" Lia cried. "Quickly!"

Max gasped as a crack opened in the seabed – a huge black ring of broken sand, running all around them. There was another rumble and a whirring sound as two enormous glass curved walls rose from the ocean floor. Before they had time to move, the glass snapped shut over their heads like a giant eyelid.

On the other side of the shield, Spike swam

frantically back and forth, knocking against the prison wall with his sword. Inside Rivet barked wildly, then lowered his head and set his propellers to full throttle. He charged at the glass, but bounced off with a dull clang. The fishing droid sank back through the water dizzily.

"Hard, Max," said the dogbot.

Lia swam to the line where the two halves of the dome met and Max followed her on his aquabike. There was a faint ridge at the join, but he couldn't get his fingers in to prise them apart. The dome had to be at least a hand-span thick.

Lia slammed her fist against the glass.

"We're trapped!" she said.

FIND THIS SPECIAL
BUMPER BOOK ON
SHELVES NOW!